victor contoski
BROKEN TREATIES

BROKEN TREATIES

victor contoski

drawings by
eriks rudans

new rivers press
1973

copyright © 1973 by victor contoski
all rights reserved
library of congress catalog card number: 72-96039
isbn 0-912284-41-2 (cloth)
       0-912284-42-0 (paper)

Special thanks to the editors of the magazines in which some of these poems first appeared:

COTTONWOOD REVIEW, DECEMBER, EPOCH, HANGING LOOSE, HARRISON STREET REVIEW, HEARSE, KAYAK, NEW POETRY OUT OF WISCONSIN, PUT POEMS, QUIXOTE, SUMAC, TAMPA POETRY REVIEW, 31 NEW AMERICAN POETS, and the roadmap edition of STROKING THE ANIMALS. "Moon Poem" appeared in PYRAMID # 5 and "Turning on Those We Love" in NORTH STONE REVIEW.

new rivers books are distributed in england by:

>philip spender
>69 randolph avenue
>london, w9, england

in the u.s. and elsewhere by:

>serendipity books
>1790 shattuck avenue
>berkeley, california
>94709

this book was manufactured in the united states for NEW RIVERS PRESS, p.o. box 578, cathedral station, new york, n.y. 10025 in a first edition of 600 copies, of which 400 have been bound in paper, 200 in cloth of which 30 have been signed and numbered by the author and the artist.

TO MY PARENTS, BROTHERS, AND WIVES

CONTENTS

I. PREPARATIONS FOR WAR

- 11 Sea
- 13 Dictionary Poem
- 15 Money
- 16 King Reason
- 17 Inanimate Object
- 18 Apple
- 19 Salt
- 21 Martyrs
- 23 My Enemy
- 24 The Jeweler
- 25 The Graduates of Harvard
- 26 The Mailman
- 27 Recital
- 28 Moles
- 29 Teachers
- 31 The God of the Old Brown Buildings
- 33 Contemporary Poets
- 35 Preparations for War
- 36 Dead Penguin
- 39 Clock
- 40 Homecoming

II. SILENCES

- 43 Silences
- 44 Moon Poem
- 45 Kansas Erotic
- 46 Those I Love
- 46 Love Poem
- 47 Cloudy Day
- 51 Moonlit Night in Kansas
- 52 Walk in the Woods
- 53 Elegy for my Name

55	Hunting Poem
57	West Wind at Lawrence
58	Nap
59	End of the Party
60	Turning on Those We Love
61	Falling Asleep
63	Dream 1971
64	Four Blessings
III.	UNKEPT PROMISES
67	Unkept Promise
68	The Mushrooms of My Dreams
69	Sequence for a Tool Box
71	Rearranging the Furniture
73	Letter
74	War Poem
77	Stepping on Pennies
78	Nocturne for the U.S. Congress
79	Elegy for a Poker Hand
82	Morning Moon
83	Teeth
85	Broken Treaty

I

PREPARATIONS FOR WAR

SEA

1

The sea inside my chest cavity
surges with the moon.

It pulls me so
I can hardly stand.

When I lie down the tide goes out,
revealing the scattered bones.

2

No one will know
     what teeth stalked this hollow.
No one will know
     what small things were devoured.

3

What has eaten
will not feed again
for some time.

Somewhere in the depths
the ravenous fish of my heart
lies hidden.

DICTIONARY POEM

1

Many many years ago
a man and a woman
both naked
got into bed
and found they had nothing
at all to say to each other.

Still naked they arose
went to their desks
and began writing a dictionary.

2

It began with *a*.
By the time it reached
the middle of the alphabet,
it was already jaded.

Yet what could it do but go on?

3

When Mary Sue used the dictionary
it wanted to close on her breasts.
But she wanted the meaning of *egregious*.

4

When the state waged war
in its name
it marched in protest
shouting: lies, lies!

But nobody recognized it.

5

As it grew older the dictionary
envied the leaves of the walnut.
It envied the distance of the stars.
It grew bitter at its own altruism.

6

One March day a man tied a string
to each corner of the dictionary.
He took it to an open field,
let out ten feet of string,
and ran as fast as he could.

The dictionary rose in the wind.
It lifted him above the clouds;
it fell on his head and killed him.

7

The man and the dictionary
were buried together.
From his grave grew a red, red rose
and from its grave a briar.

8

But the dictionary did not die.

It rose from its grave at the full moon,
entered the library through an open window
and settled in the poetry section.

Each night it lay on a different book
kissing it and sucking its blood
until the librarian found out.

He buried the dictionary in the reference room
with a stake through its heart.

MONEY

At first it will seem tame,
willing to be domesticated.

It will nest
in your pocket
or curl up in a corner
reciting softly to itself
the names of the presidents.

It will delight your friends,
shake hands with men
like a dog and lick
the legs of women.

But like an amoeba
it makes love
in secret
only to itself.

Fold it frequently;
it needs exercise.

Water it every three days
and it will repay you
with displays of affection.

Then one day when you think
you are its master
it will turn its head
as if for a kiss
and bite you gently
on the hand.

There will be no pain
but in thirty seconds
the poison will reach your heart

KING REASON

        My heart went begging.

        Have you no shame?

        Please, sir, it's not for myself.
        But King Reason sits all day
        in his tower blind as a bat
        imagining his kingdoms.
                                Give
        him a crust of bread.

INANIMATE OBJECT

1

A black hole
like a waterless well
the width of a man's body,
the inanimate object
refreshes no one.

2

Years ago
I dropped affection
in it
like a stone.

For forty years
I have held my breath
listening
for the rock
to hit bottom.

APPLE

        This twisted tree was once
        a beautiful young girl.
        Now she has grown old.

        She offers me a cold kiss.

        I take it on my tongue, saying:
        This is my body.

SALT

1

Salt spilled
on the wooden table.

Its crystals lie
like fallen snow.

Soon it will enter the wood
which will never bloom again.

2

The butcher sweats like a pig.
He covers himself with blood.
After work his clothes dry in the sun.

Salt turns them white.

He puts them back on and goes to the park
where he mounts a huge pedestal
thinking the people pay him homage.

But they are honoring salt.

3

A king's daughter
who worked for a witch
made salt with her tears.

She cried every day
till she filled a pail.

Put the tears of a princess
on your mashed potatoes.

4

Salt lies deep underground
like those we love.

Dirty men dig down
to stand amazed at its beauty.

They carve it into statues:
Christ at the Last Supper,
the Virgin Mary,
St. John of the Depths.

Then they leave their work
to the moisture of centuries.

But in the light of day
they can no longer worship
in high stone churches.

5

My first communion:

far down under the earth
someone placed on my tongue
a pinch of salt.

MARTYRS

        Their fear:
            the Kind of Pleasure
            claims them as his own.
            He has come to ransom them.

MY ENEMY

His face is hidden in the closet
where for years he has stored
the bodies of women.

When the sun goes down
I hear him in his cellar
sharpening knives.

Now he invites me to dinner
saying blood is thicker than water,
saying that he is my brother.

THE JEWELER

> Show me what you love,
> said the jeweler,
> and I will show you
> stone,
> stone.

THE GRADUATES OF HARVARD

Their competent hands are
poised above the buttons.
Their steps in the corridors
ring with justice.

Though they are silent
their faces show
that God has appeared to them.

He has fixed the blood in their veins
and set tradition upon them like a halo.
He has blessed their endeavors with money
and strewn His poor about their feet like flowers.

THE MAILMAN

In the dark of night
he has opened what is mine
looking for money
and copying excerpts
for his novel.

For years he has
burned my mail in secret
trying to make me believe
my friends have forgotten me.

RECITAL

In the great hall
surrounded by sages
we heard the poet
speak of betrayals
and bestiality,
undress our wives
and put our daughters
through all the various
positions of love.

We heard them gasp
at our sides,
saw fingers tremble
on polished wood
and lithe bodies strain
in satin bondage.

And when he finished
their delicate hands
set thunder loose.

We knew then we could
never satisfy them
and men with horns
smelling of goat
would visit them
in their dreams.

MOLES

Their paths lead
to the graves of those we love.
Only the blind can follow them.

TEACHERS

1

At dawn
they hoist their banners
proclaiming *Virtue and Honor*
in a dead language.

They set out along the road
called Justice
that has no signs.

Their coats make them
invisible to all
but the pure-in-heart.

Their dusty shoes
with the magic holes
leap centuries.

They are looking for dragons.

2

Along the way
they compile dictionaries
and reference grammars
noting in particular
    the past
    the present
    the future-perfect.

The execution of the poor they record
under *poor* and *execution*,
the rape of the innocent
under *money*.

Every now and then
they rescue beautiful naked women
who never even notice them.

3

At evening they return home
tired
to their cold porridge.

Their hearts beat
loud
as clocks.

Listlessly
they kiss
their gold gray wives,

and flop down in easy chairs,
their laps full
of critical articles.

4

At ten o'clock
their lights go out.

Nothing kisses them
like a vampire.

And monsters
chew their bones
in darkness.

THE GOD OF THE OLD BROWN BUILDINGS

The whites of his eyes
are like dirty snow

as he squats forever
on his withered haunches

the god of the old brown buildings.

While careless traditional deities
hallow the groves

he sits before you
like an obscene mountain

his head in his grimy hands.

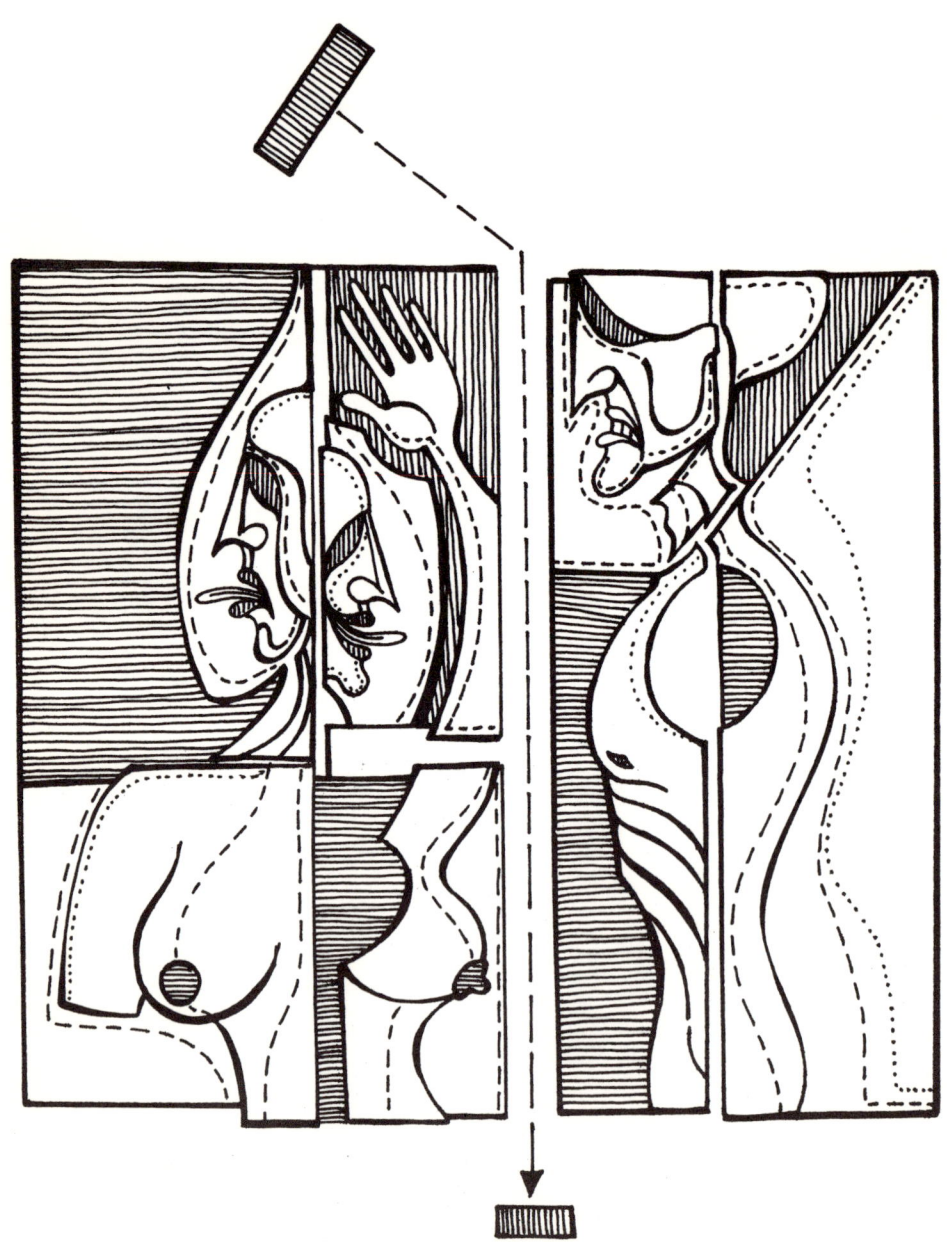

CONTEMPORARY POETS

1

They stare out at me
from their photographs
as if I were to blame
for the state of poetry.

They are all younger than I am.   Or older.
More innocent.   Or more experienced.
More beautiful and more intense.

"Our lives," say their biographies,
"are better than yours, fuller.
We are not happy with your shallow happiness;
but in our work we have a fierce joy
that you can never know.

"There is a parallel world to yours.
We step into it whenever we want to.
It clothes us in light."

2

I take the pictures in my hands,
shuffle them, and lay them out,
seven in a row.

The rules are simple:
men on women or women on men;
bearded men are wild:
they go on anybody;
lesbians go in the center:
you build on them
because they are so beautiful.

Out of all those moves,
you'd think there would be one.

But I'm stuck again.

PREPARATIONS FOR WAR

By the sixth of December
there had been no stars for a week.

Rumors came of advances and withdrawals.
Two children were frozen in the woods,
and everybody said it was an omen.
A vagabond came through with only one eye.
We offered friendship, fire,
and even our daughters,
but we would not stay.

Winter gathered his armies
throughout the Northlands.

By the sixth of December we knew.

The grass went underground,
and the wind walked all night in the attic.

DEAD PENGUIN

1

Christmas.
Madison, Wisconsin.
On my doorstep
lies a penguin
fat and dead
like Santa Claus.

2

There are no nail holes in the hands
and no nail holes in the feet.
There is no bullet mark
in his white belly.

Only around his beak
a small trickle of black blood
as if his tongue still held
the taste of something
too bitter to be borne.

3

His widow feels the tears drop
one by one
on her dirty white belly.

His young son
wipes the black blood
from the hard lips
of his father.

His beautiful daughter
the one all young penguins
want to marry
feels the ice pulse
under her feet like a heart.

4

The animals gather
like magi.

Their gifts are themselves:
the chipmunk his terror,
the wolf his pity,
the eagle his appetite.

The monkey hides his face
in a handkerchief
and nobody knows
if he's laughing or crying.

5

A priest steps forward
carrying the censor
on his webbed feet
like an egg.

"Having obeyed the laws
of God and Wisconsin,
this penguin passed over with honor.
May God take him
to a place colder
than Antarctica
and full of fish."

6

Far off to one side
stands the zoo keeper
ashamed.

The hand that holds the whip
is clenched into a fist.
Its white knuckles shine
like the belly of a penguin.

CLOCK

Who looks at a clock will find
the white reflection of his face.

His eyes have gone,
his nose and ears.

His hair has fallen,
his mouth becomes numerals

as he returns at 5:30
to stand before a mirror

which announces: behold
the egg has come home.

HOMECOMING

Back to the books.

And my old master, Pain,
greeted me with open arms.

Didn't I tell you?
    he said.
What have you gained?

Rivers still flow like blood;
air stops the mouth like a pillow;
the world is spun
like a child in blind man's bluff.

But I had plans
    I told him.
I kept telling myself this story,
one with a happy ending,
saying the words over and over
till they lost their meaning.

What did you expect,
    he said,
        love from the stone?
        justice from the water?

Welcome home,
    said the old master, Pain.

II

SILENCES

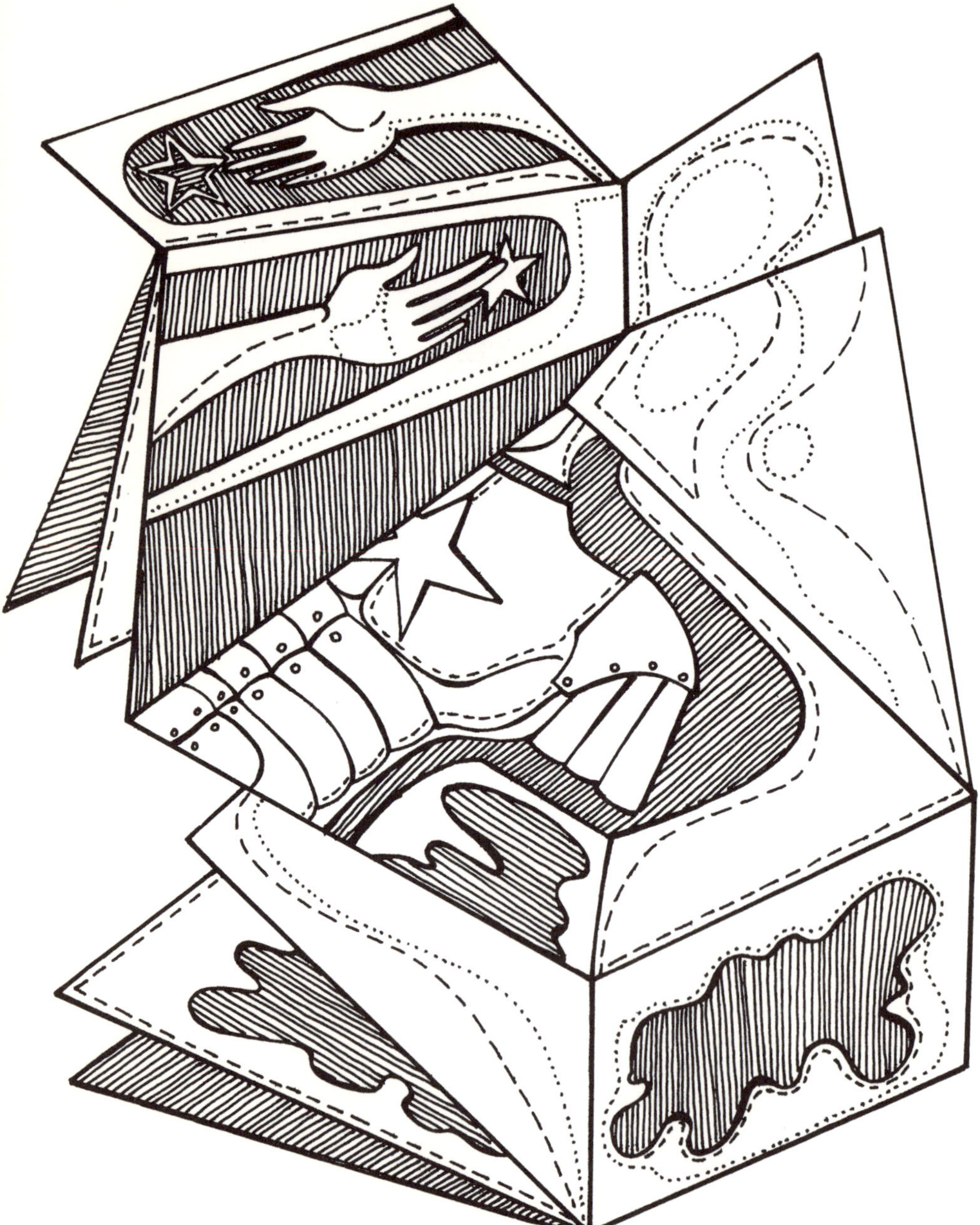

SILENCES

1

Waiting for hope
the beautiful
have gone dumb.

It died
in a foreign country.

2

All night long
the moon has been calling:
come.   come.

The suicide hears
the voice of his love.

MOON POEM

The moon is a beautiful barren woman.
When she enters the room all eyes turn to her.
One would think she has no sorrow.

KANSAS EROTIC

A husband and wife
sleep in each other's arms
in the middle of Kansas.

Content overhead
Cepheus and Cassiopeia
have not moved the whole night.

The wind has gone east
looking for someone to love.

Embarrassed by the silence
the air-conditioner lurches
into a rough lullaby it learned
thousands of years ago
from an ogre who loved a princess.

THOSE I LOVE

>Those I love—
>even in my dreams
>I see only their backs.
>
>O, let me be there
>with them
>in a far country
>
>away from the hanging tongues
>and the sheep faces
>of those that love me.

LOVE POEM

>Because of you
>I do nothing.
>
>You have sewn pockets
>around my hands.

CLOUDY DAY

1

It is cold for April
yesterday snow fell

the trees are still bare
the ground is crumpled

on such a day
a man dies.

2

The dirty dishes
wait in the sink
like judgement

the record is still turning
but no music comes

I'd turn off the phonograph
if I could move.

3

For a long time now
I have been sitting
before the window

there is dust on my hands.

4

Look at the clouds
it has been threatening
for some time

some say rain
some say war.

5

O love

if we had lips
we could kiss

if we had a drink
there's no telling
what we could do.

6

Yesterday
I cleaned out my desk

it will never
be cluttered again

no more dust
will form on my poems
and nobody will ever move them.

7

My neighbor is in his garage
pounding nails

one blow an hour
like a slow pendulum

he is working
as usual
on his coffin

he is in no hurry

at the rate he is going
he will finish
in a thousand years.

8

Somewhere far away
in gold and silver
a king is marching
to muffled trumpets.

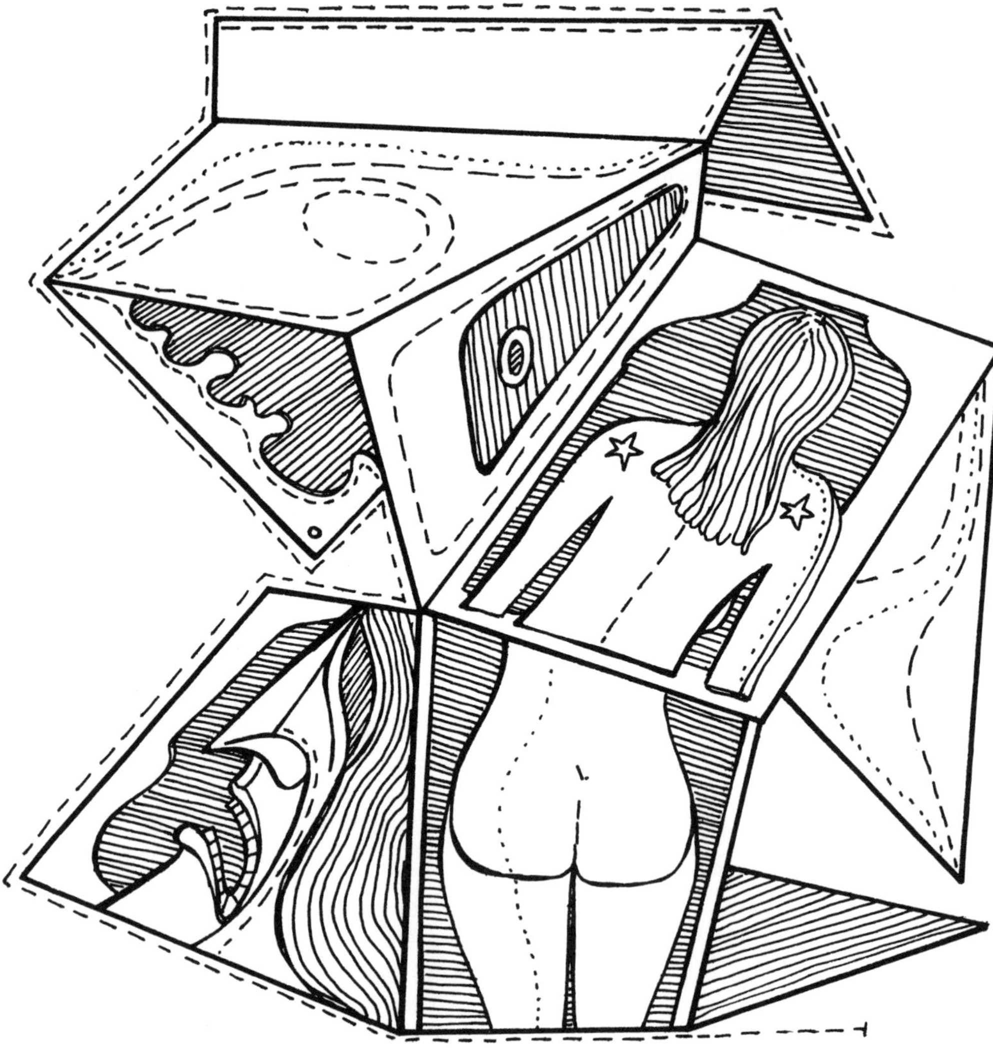

MOONLIT NIGHT IN KANSAS

The plains of Kansas stretch out
under the moon like a sheet of music.

Buffalo lie bleeding in the grass.
The sound of their panting
rolls along the Kaw River
like the beat of a ghostly tom-tom.

Arcturus descends
andante molto cantabile.

The sons of the homesteaders
have migrated to Asia.

Their daughters went east
to enter the Miss America Pageant
and were never heard from again.

An old Indian recites
meaningless words:
Topeka, Manhattan, Wichita.

WALK IN THE WOODS

        For the love of wood
        I kneel down
        and offer it my hands.

        If I am very still
        and wait a long time
        bark will grow over them.

ELEGY FOR MY NAME

               1

My name has gone into the forest
leaving its trail of bread crumbs.

It has walked naked
into the camp of the enemy
trusting a flag.

O my name
my name.

Birds have eaten the way back.
Soldiers of the emperor surround you.

               2

The native have
    broken your thumbs
        pierced your eyeballs with their pins
      attached wires to your genitals.

They have dispersed
the letters of my name.

O my name
my name.

3

My name
    fallen among savages
My name
    a toy on the lips
    of the emperor's wives
My name
    its flesh devoured
    its bones gnawed in the forest

My name
    that gave me what it had
My name
    that leaves not even itself behind it

Children play football with my name.

4

Yet it was true.
Tortured, it told nothing.

It died
calling
me.

HUNTING POEM

Yesterday I left
footprints in the snow
as I went to the mailbox.

During the night something
crossed my path.   Its footprints
cannot be found in any book.

I began to follow them
but the snow is blinding.

I close my eyes and follow in darkness
the track of an unknown animal.

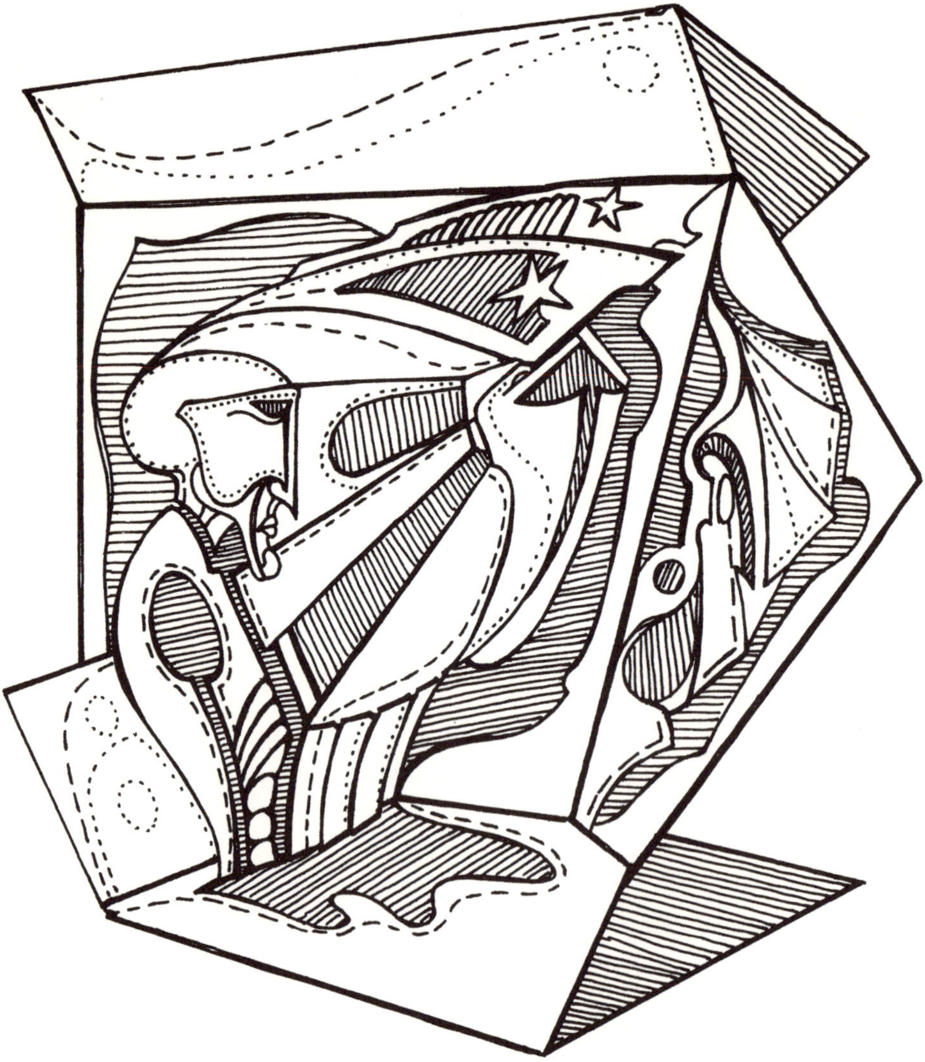

WEST WIND AT LAWRENCE

At midnight, late June
in Lawrence, Kansas,
the west wind wanders in
over the plains
from Manhattan and Topeka
like a violin lost
in the slow movement
of a Russian concerto.

I look toward Cassiopeia
and pray for Dmitri Shostakovich
saying:
> *Caph*
> *Schedar*
> *Navi*
> *Ruchbah.*

NAP

          1

I have been reading so long
my eyes are tired.

I put the book
back in its cage.

My library is sullen.
The books refuse to eat.

Not one has ever
reproduced in captivity.

The words dream listlessly
of the veldt where they were born.

          2

My eyes close.
I lie down on my back.

The girl of my dreams
bends over my body.

Her name is Darkness.
She is a vampire.

Her lips on my neck are softer
than anything I know.

END OF THE PARTY

Streetlights go off singing
at the tops of their voices.
Orion, too drunk to drive,
is helped to a taxi.

The Fritos and Corn-snips
have gone for a moonlight walk
and just disappeared.
So has the whiskey.

Dirt came late, uninvited,
but helped entertain the guests.
Now he takes formal possession
of the living room.

The neighbors (thank goodness)
have been dead for years.

The tired house goes around
turning off lights.
Empty glasses pair off
in dark corners.

Overhead the moon
keeps running to the bathroom.

•

TURNING ON THOSE WE LOVE

The way a gnarled hand turns a knob to an empty room.
The way an ugly girl turns toward her mirror.

The way a car turns from the wrong lane.
The way the road turns toward the desert.

The way a dead fish turns up its white belly in the water.
The way a hunter turns with a bird in his sights.
The way a circus lion turns on the man with the whip.

The way an innocent man turns to face his accuser.
The way a judge turns toward a man he will sentence.
The way a prisoner turns toward the wall.

The way a bullet turns in the barrel as it leaps toward the light.

The way the hands of a clock turn, joyless and certain.
The way Orion turns in the clear autumn sky.

FALLING ASLEEP

A flock of birds flies
slowly over your head.
Each one has a broken wing.

Slowly the house
is filling up with snow.

Your breath is heavy
as a freight train
falling off a bridge.

It is your body falling.

The hands of the dead
reach out to catch you.

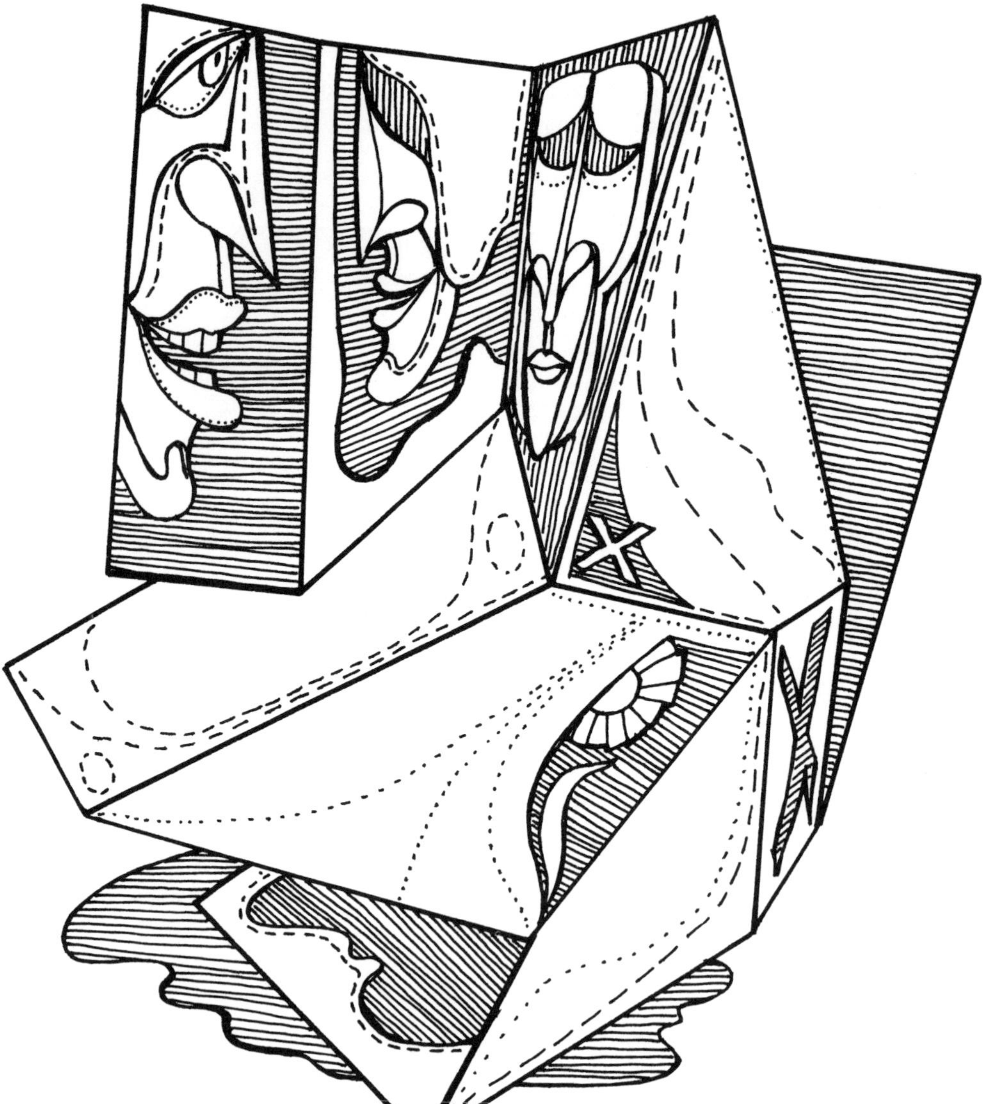

DREAM 1971

At 5:10 a.m. Uncle Henry
came back from the dead
still partially bald
his face a round red sun
his fists full of cards.

I thought he had answers
shoving his hands toward me.

He had just one question:
what do you do
with cards like these?

FOUR BLESSINGS
   (for Herb and Ginny Smith)

1. When the beautiful die
   may you be there
   to comfort the mourners.

2. May your fingers never close.

3. When giant corporations
   surround your house
   like beasts in the night
   may you be spirited away to safety.

4. May the letters of the alphabet
   hold you and keep you
   forever and ever. Amen.

III

UNKEPT PROMISES

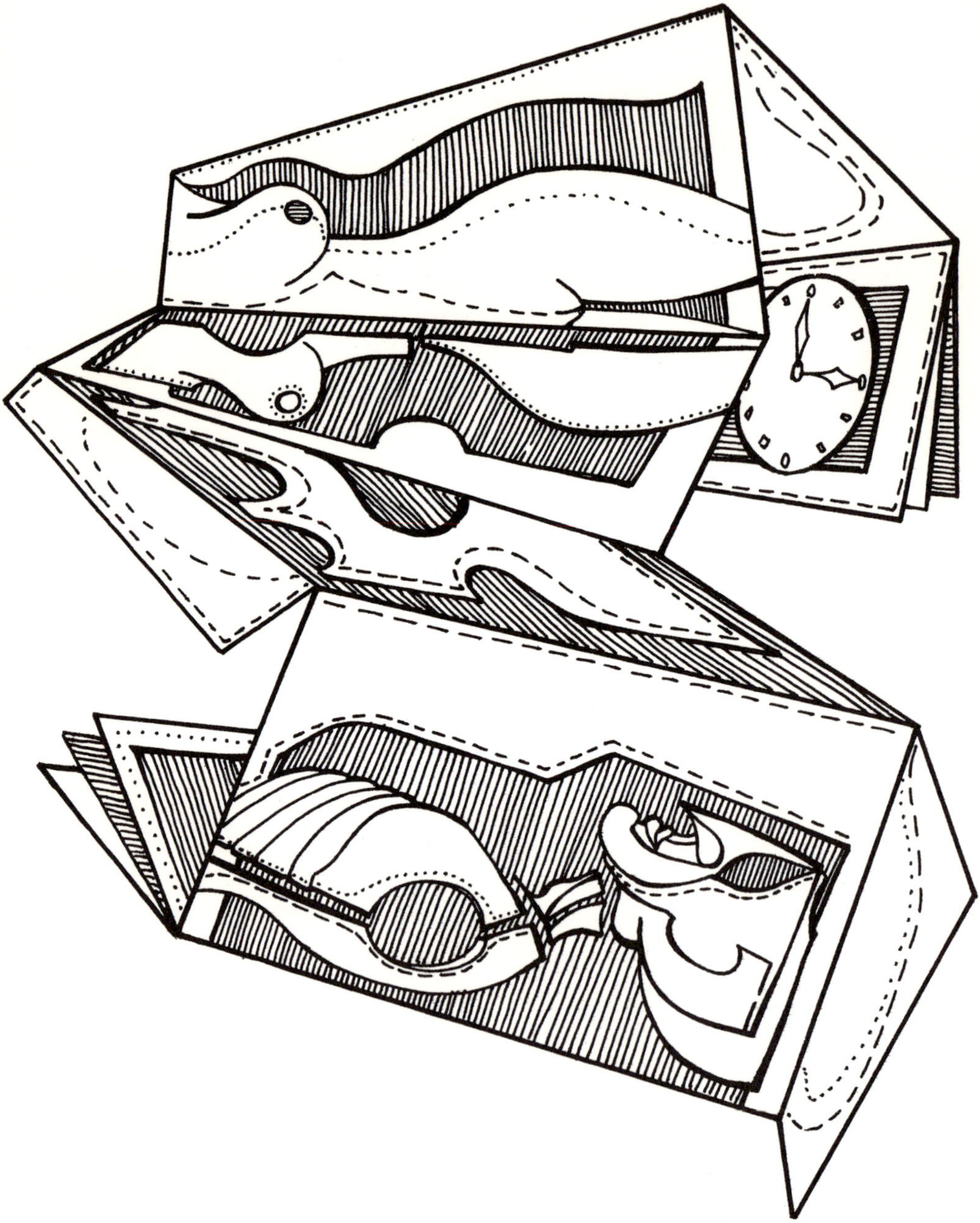

UNKEPT PROMISES

It was rotting in the wall
for months like a mouse
caught in the hidden wire
and executed offhand.

Gagging we gingerly
took it out in pieces
with pliers and threw
the hunks in the garbage.

Then we opened windows.

But the wall
will never be clean again.

THE MUSHROOMS OF MY DREAMS

1

The mushrooms of my dreams
stand like fierce young girls
under the eyes of soldiers.

Though they are the colors of the rainbow
to the poor they look white as bread.

They cluster in bunches
all over the fields of sleep.

2

Come morning I seek them in books.

Their names
are the beautiful names
of foreign women.

I recognize their pictures.

Such mushrooms, read the captions,
grow only in the dreams of certain poets.

They are poison, poison, poison.

SEQUENCE FOR A TOOL BOX

1

Hammer

I come
weighed down with weapons.

From each hand
hangs a hammer.

Their lifeless arcs
swing like grey moons

from my past
to my future.

Nothing dances
to the heft of their music

as I lay their dull, heavy heads
on the breasts of the woman I love.

2

Pliers

The steel beak
searches for something to twist.

Through clenched teeth
it sings of nothing human.

3

Saw

High above the sound
of its voice

it hears the wood weeping.

4

Plane

The tongue of the plane
falls silent.

In the service of Jack
it shaved the legs of the princess
caressed her
without tenderness
lopped ten pounds off her hips
smoothed the backs of her hands
to make her worthy
of a blacksmith's son.

Now
it licks wood
air
water
rust

and dreams
of the flesh of a girl.

REARRANGING THE FURNITURE

I don't like the wall, she said.
Knock it down.

True to my vows
I set my hammer to work
no questions asked.

Is it done?

Not yet.

Hurry up.

Now it's finished.
Look:
    the house is tottering.

but she ran out crying:
freedom! freedom!

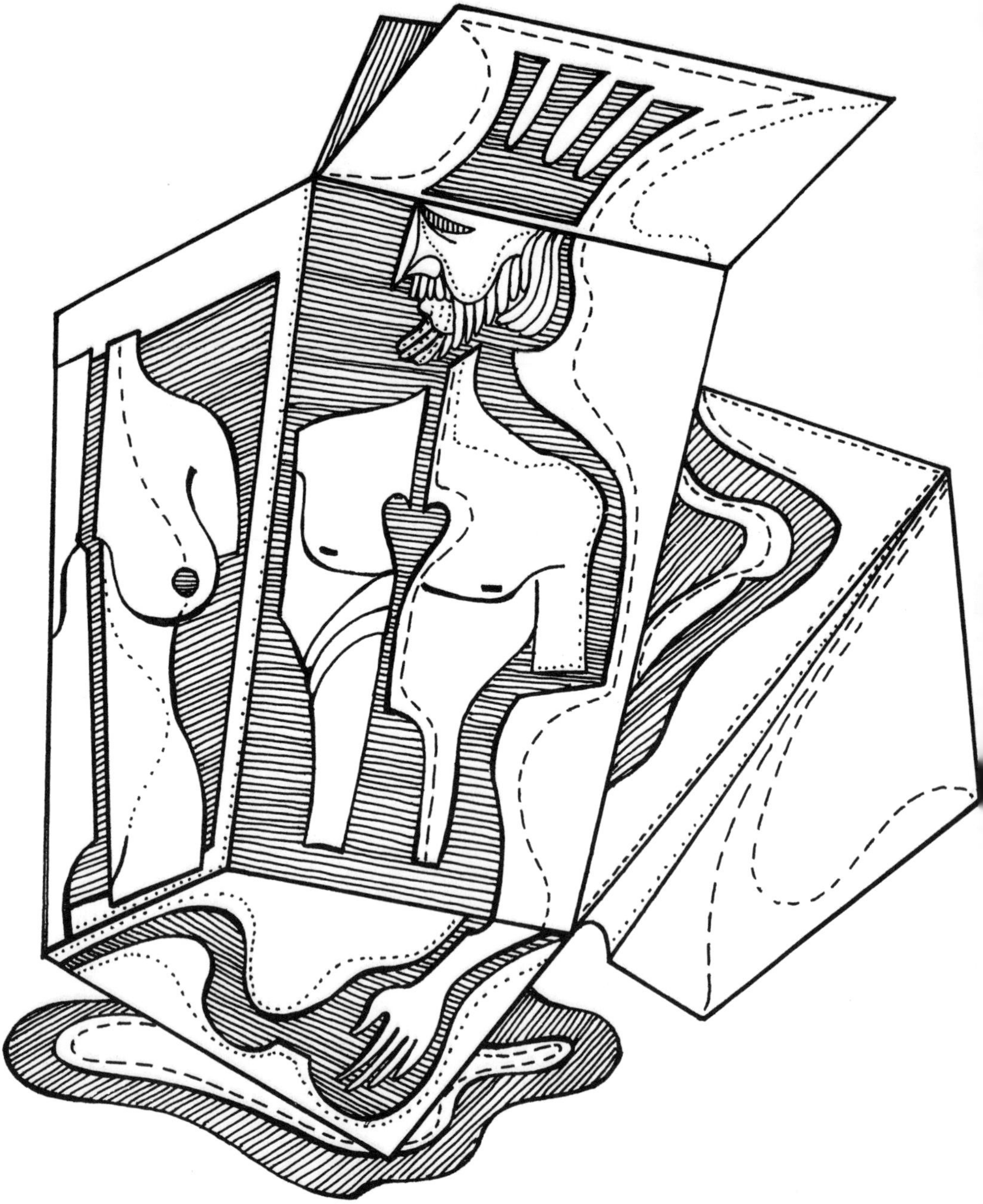

LETTER

You left behind you
a black book in the corner
The Story of Ancient Civilizations

tales of butcher-heroes
maimed captives
women weeping
and God
lapping the blood
of his children

hope you like your job
in the new country

just thought I'd tell you
it's still here
gathering dust
in the ruins

that black book.

WAR POEM

1

The generals have spent the evening
looking at stars and dreaming of dark women.

Their wives are bravely dying of cancer.
Their sons have been massacred.

Night descends huge as an airplane.
Let the generals sleep.

2

All day long congressmen have been weeping
for the lovers of their unfaithful wives,

for the mathematicians counting the enemy dead,
for small things that moved in the underbrush,

for the country beautiful as a girl's body
that proved too powerful for her dreams.

3

A light burns late at the White House.
The president is at his desk writing poetry.

The vice-president thumbs through Roget's thesaurus.
The secretary of state checks the Library of Congress.

The president looks far out into the night
beyond the stars seeking an adjective.

4

Moonlight falls on the half-opened lips
of a sleeping girl in Omaha, Nebraska.

Her breasts, full as the moon, move slowly
as a night patrol through strange territory.

The ghost of Thomas Jefferson comes in through the window.
He bends over her body, and she does not wake.

All night he drinks the pure fresh blood
of a young virgin from Omaha, Nebraska.

5

At the other end of the world in Warren, Ohio,
the streetlights stagger like drunken soldiers.

The town sleeps.   Protestants breathe in.
Catholics breathe out.   Nobody snores.

Only an evil old lady lies awake
hoping her only son will die.

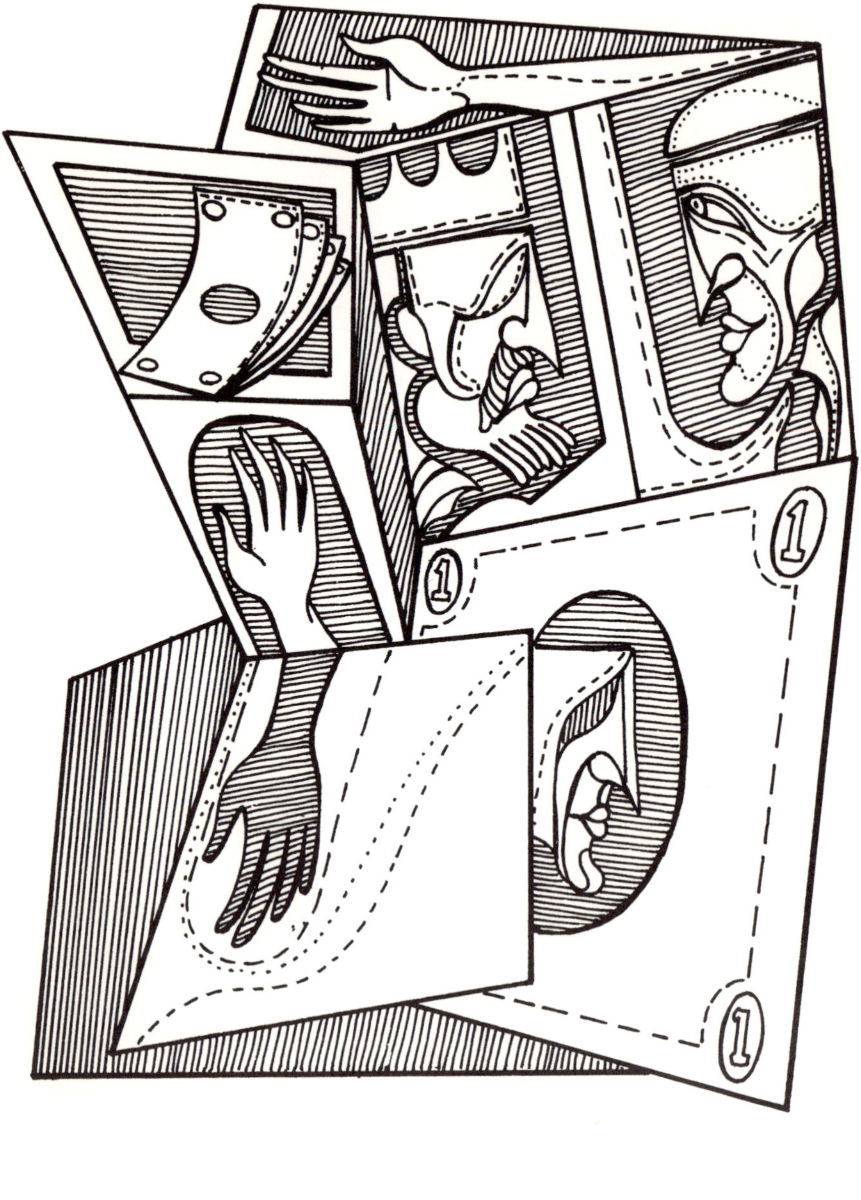

STEPPING ON PENNIES

When you step on a penny
you smear the date.
You rub *God* out of
In God We Trust.
No one can read *liberty*
after you have stepped
on a penny.

When you step on a penny
you plant a seed
that will sprout in a museum,
an unknown metal
picturing a strange man
with the mark of a boot
on his face.

NOCTURNE FOR THE U.S. CONGRESS

Shadows fall like men
on the steps of the U.S. Senate Building.

The sun goes down over the House of Representatives
like a motion to discuss secret wars in Asia.

The janitor turns out the lights one by one.
He searches the empty washrooms for bombs.

The urine of our elected representatives
disappears like the young.   It goes underground
where it mingles with the urine of the poor
and the statesman-like urine of the president
and the pale virtuous urine of the first lady.

Oh, it is night
when taxes ripen like grapes.

It is night for the Department of Commerce.
It is night for the United States Treasury.
It is night for the Ways and Means Committee.

The pure stars march across the heavens
of Washington D.C. like armies.

And darkness descends on the Department of Justice.

ELEGY FOR A POKER HAND

1

The Four of Hearts
Someone has been lying about America
all these years—saying it is the land
of justice, idealism, and freedom;
that it is the land of opportunity
where any boy can grow up to be president.

Lies: all of them.
They come from the mouth of the dealer
who has just given you the four of hearts.

2

The Jack of Clubs
The jack of clubs is like an early guest,
ill-at-ease, doesn't know anybody, hard to talk to.
He keeps apologizing and looking at his watch,
wondering when the others will come.

And you know already it will be a lousy party.

3

The Six of Diamonds
The six of diamonds is not happy with you either.
Who could guess that it dreams
of being carried in the pocket
of John Carter, Warlord of Mars,
as he roams the dead sea bottoms
and mysterious cities of Barsoom?

4

The Deuce of Spades
Pornographic decks
feature pictures of naked lovers
in various positions.

Gamblers never notice
their young bodies.

They look
—as you do—
at the two of spades.

5

The Ten of Diamonds
Red dye is dangerous.

A condemned murderer
cuts out the red spots on his cards
like the hearts of his victims.

He soaks them
and wads them tightly
in a fountain pen cap,

stuffs in
a small piece of steel.

He heats the cap,
bending his head over it
like a priest at consecration.

The ten of diamonds
blows his brains out.

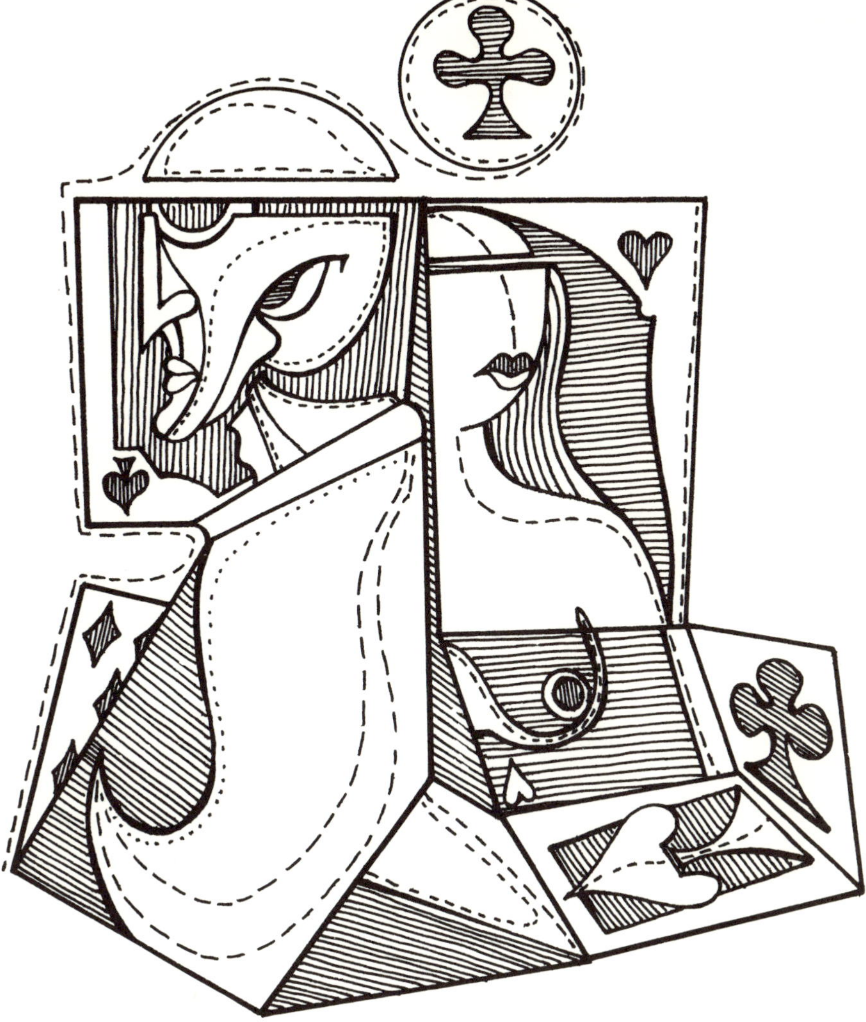

MORNING MOON

The barbarians in the hills
are sharpening their weapons.

All night the ghosts of Indians
have been reeling through darkness

drinking their courage,
their faces smeared with grief.

The drum of the blood
takes up its message.

The full moon hangs low
over Madison, Wisconsin,

like a chip from a statue
of an ancient civilization.

Yellow as from age.
Red as from fire.

TEETH

1

Kiss the one you love.
Behind the lips
teeth are waiting

like a man with a weapon
waits in a dark alley.

2

They are not knives
but clubs.

They come down on meat
like a lead pipe
on the head of a woman.

3

Sometimes in dreams
they wither and turn soft
like rotten cactus.

They curl up and fall out
like men refusing to fight
an unpopular war.

4

If you are beaten long enough and hard enough
your teeth will be knocked out.

Then you can use them as chessmen:
front teeth, pawns;
back teeth, pieces.

5

They line up in the mouth
like soldiers for inspection.

Ever since I can remember
they have surrounded the tongue,

reminding what is soft
of what is hard.

BROKEN TREATY

        These words
        written in trust
        lie now
        shaming
        the good white paper.

PS   Contoski, Victor.
3553
O5.4   Broken treaties.
B7

**NORMANDALE
COMMUNITY COLLEGE**
9700 France Avenue South
Bloomington, Minnesota 55431